Pageant Paige Takes the Stage

By Michelle Hall-Lessard
Illustrated by Caterina Cacciagrani

ISBN: 9798832217079

Editor: Bryson Taylor Publishing
Publisher: Bryson Taylor Publishing

Dedication

**This book is dedicated to my children Paige and Chase.
May you always have a passion in and for life.**

Bryson Taylor Publishing
a division of Bryson Taylor Inc.

It all began in grade number two.

This little girl Paige had no activity to do.

Her Mom would say activities are a way to make friends and have fun.

But nothing she tried would get the job done.

Her Mom exposed endless choices to try.

But little Miss Paige would only sulk and cry.

Paige always wanted to be the star of whatever she did.

She was like no other ordinary kid.

Everyone said that she "beats to her own drum."

Her personality was even too much for some.

She wore high heels of plastic that would clunk down the hall. Her teacher thought it was distracting and was worried she could fall.

Her head was held high, and her outfits were bright, full of bling. She sported fancy outfits, glossy nail polish, necklaces, and a shiny ring.

Her friend Gabby loved soccer. So, a game, she would see. She said, "The kids just run back and forth. This sport is not for me!"

To dance class, she went to try ballet and tap.

It was so difficult for her to shuffle or flap.

"This is not my thing. I have no rhythm or grace.

I know in my heart this is just not my place".

She would go to karate each week to watch her brother, Chase.

"I might as well try it if I need to be in this space."

Karate was yet another attempt to find love.

She learned to kick, grapple, and push down with a shove.

She mastered the number one pinion and earned a yellow belt.

Although it should be fun - she knew how she felt.

Scouting was a place to sell cookies, earn badges, and sleep in a tent.

Her mom being the leader, was the only reason she went.

Cheerleading was a new adventure on deck.

All of this tumbling and jumping would cause such a wreck.

Playing the flute would sound pretty and soft.

This would become a challenge with notes going aloft.

One day to a pageant she went to see.

"I think I found just the right passion for me!"

Each contestant rocked the runway in an outfit with style.

They walked with purpose, hit poses, and ended with a smile.

Then the contestants wore gowns and were graceful as can be.

"I want to wear a gown - I want that to be me."

These girls helped others and interviewed well.

"I want to try this. I can tell."

Paige signed up for a pageant in her hometown in Maine.

The excitement for pageant day was too much to explain.

The interview was fun when answering about the things she loves to do—clam digging, downhill skiing, and volunteering too.

The fun fashion was where she could walk like a star.

She twirled, hit her poses, and was really on par.

Her gown was beautiful, and she felt like a queen.

As everyone watched, she finally felt seen.

The pageants brought Paige lots of joy and confidence as well.

There was no other activity that could even parallel.

Crowning time was here, and her dreams all came true.

Pageants are just what she wanted to do.

About the Author

Michelle Hall Lessard is a graduate of the University of Maryland with a B.A. in dance and a graduate of the University of Southern Maine, where she received her Masters of Science in Education. She holds a K-8 elementary education and a special education certificate and is in her 15th year of teaching elementary school.

As a dance instructor, she has training in tap, modern, jazz, ballet, hip hop, and West African dance. Michelle was the director and owner of City Dance studios for 25 years with Falmouth, South Portland, and Biddeford, Maine, locations. She has taught grades 2, 4, Kindergarten, and Functional Life Skills in special education (with most of her years in kindergarten). She is currently a Kindergarten teacher at Alfred Elementary School in Alfred, Maine.

Michelle is 2022, Ms. Maine, for American Women Pageants, and has been involved in pageantry for many years. Her love for literature, education, pageants, and volunteering merged into one, leading her to empower girls and young women to be their best through coaching, directing, and choreographing pageants.

About the Illustrator

Caterina Cacciagrani is an illustrator, artist, studio potter, and ceramics instructor in the Boston area. She received her Bachelor of Arts in Music, with a concentration in Renaissance History from the University of Maine and earned a Masters of Science in Environmental Studies from Antioch in Keene, NH. *Pageant Paige* is her second children's book, preceded by *Summer's Shadow* in 2021. She is focusing on her pottery career, including hand-crafted custom designs. Caterina travels and sells her creations at various retail art/craft shows in New England, teaches private and group pottery and ceramic classes, and creates her commissioned custom pieces for clients.

Made in the USA
Middletown, DE
17 August 2022

71336788R00015